Little Hymns™

Little Hymns • O' Little Town of Bethlehem
Written and illustrated by Andy Holmes
Watercolor by Cameron Thorp and Matt Taylor
Music transcription by Marty Franks

Copyright ©1992 by HSH Educational Media Company
P.O. Box 167187, Irving, Texas 75016

All rights reserved. No part of this book may be reproduced or transmitted in any form or by any means, electronic or mechanical, including photocopying, recording, or by any information storage and retrieval systems without prior written permission from the publisher.

First Printing 1992
ISBN 0-929216-51-2
Printed in the United States of America

Published by

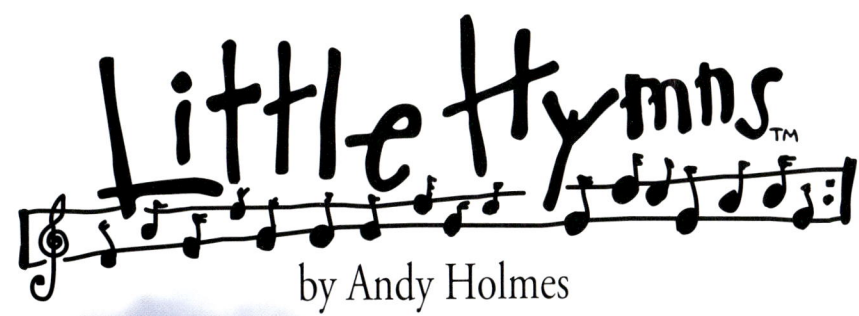

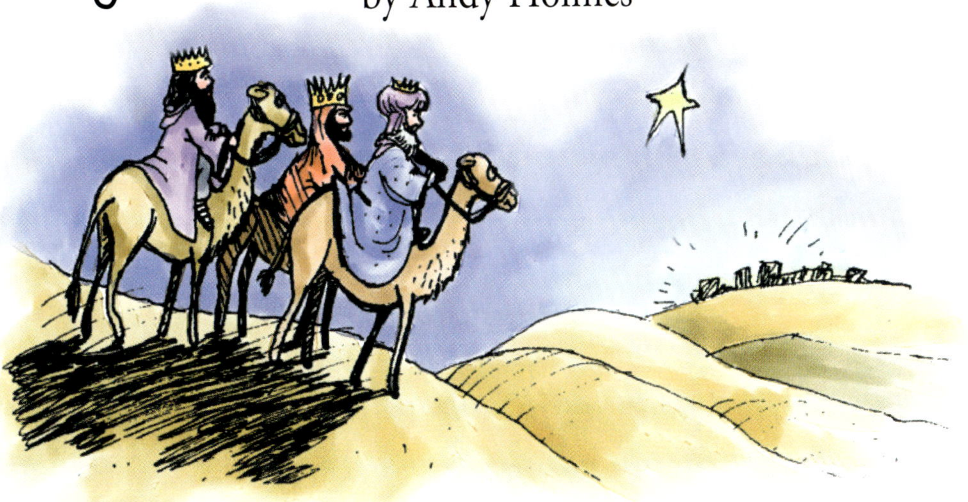

O Little Town Of Bethlehem

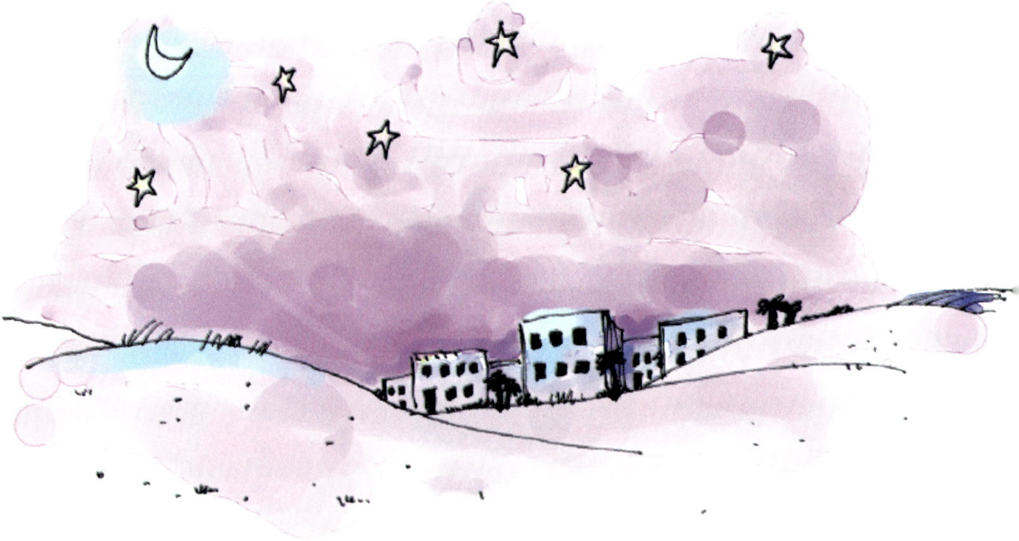

O lit-tle town of Beth-le-hem, how still we see thee lie!

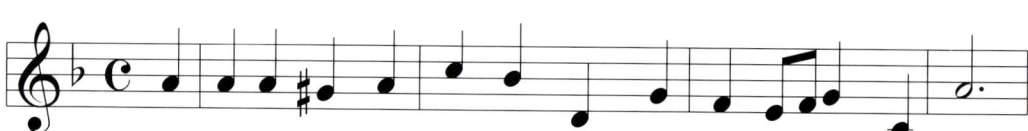

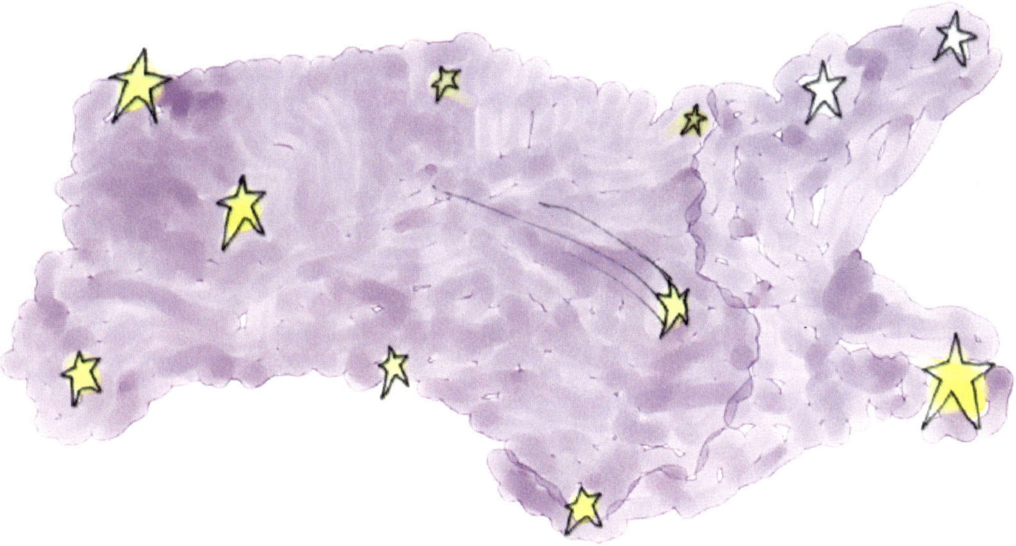

A-bove thy deep and dream-less sleep the si-lent stars go by.

Yet in thy dark streets shin-eth the ev-er-last-ing light.

For Christ is born of Ma - ry, and gath-ered all a- bove,

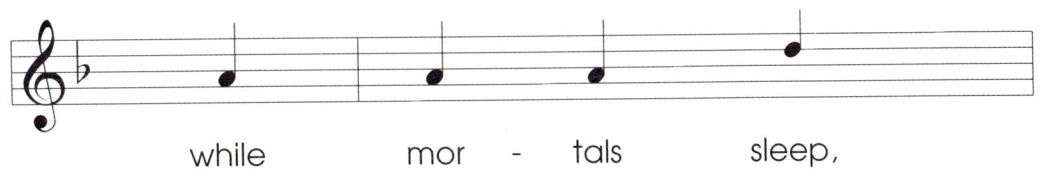

the an-gels keep their watch of won-dering love.

O morn - ing stars to - geth - er,

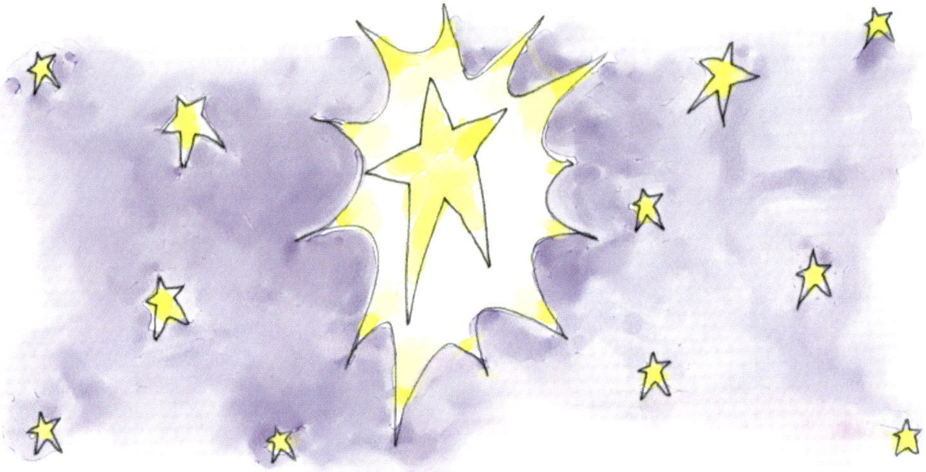

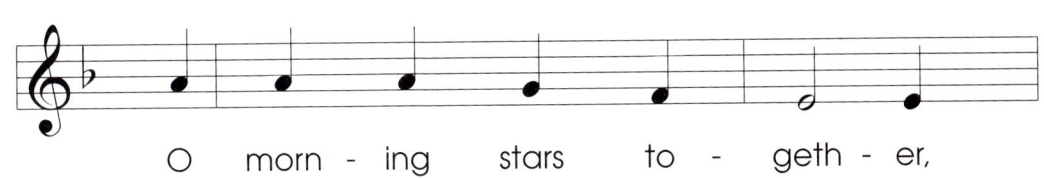

pro - claim the ho - ly birth,

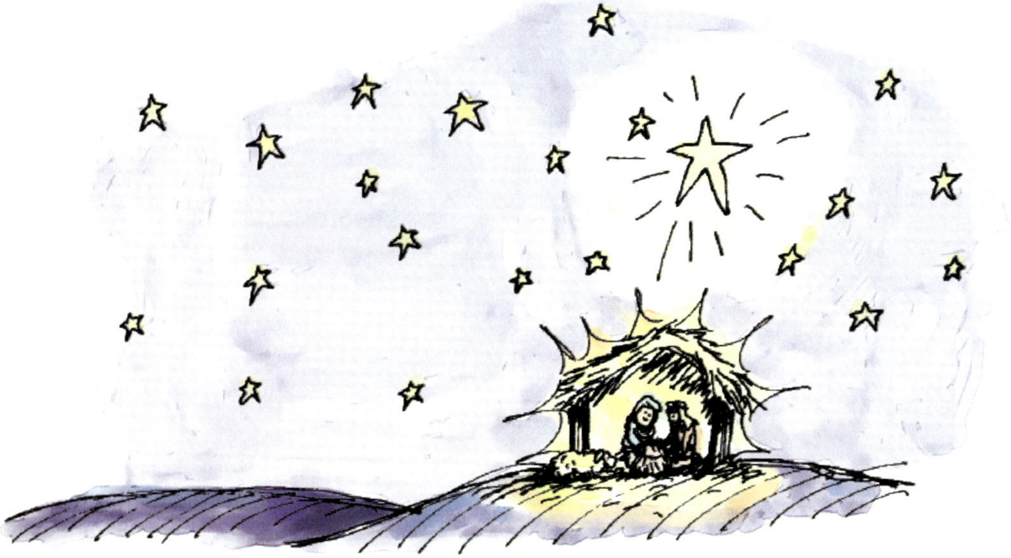

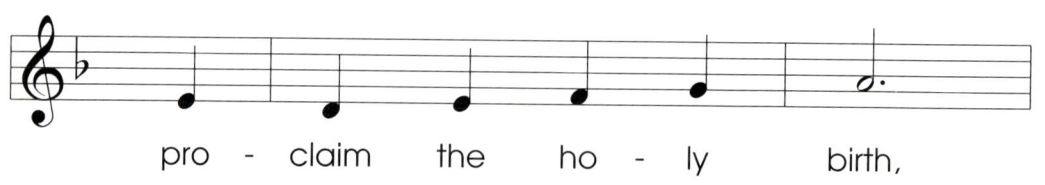

so God im-parts to hu-man hearts the bless-ings of His heaven.

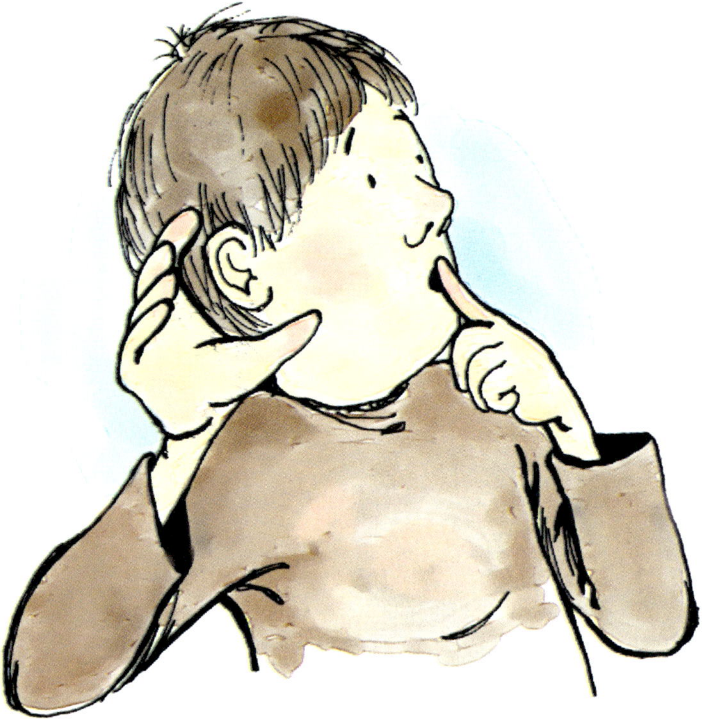

No ear may hear His com- ing, but in this world of sin

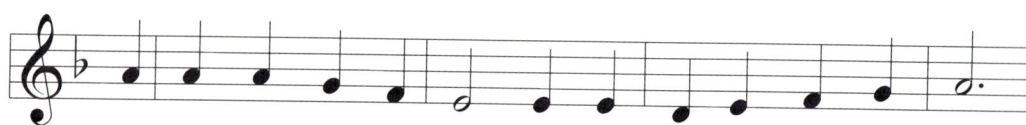

the dear Christ en - ters in.

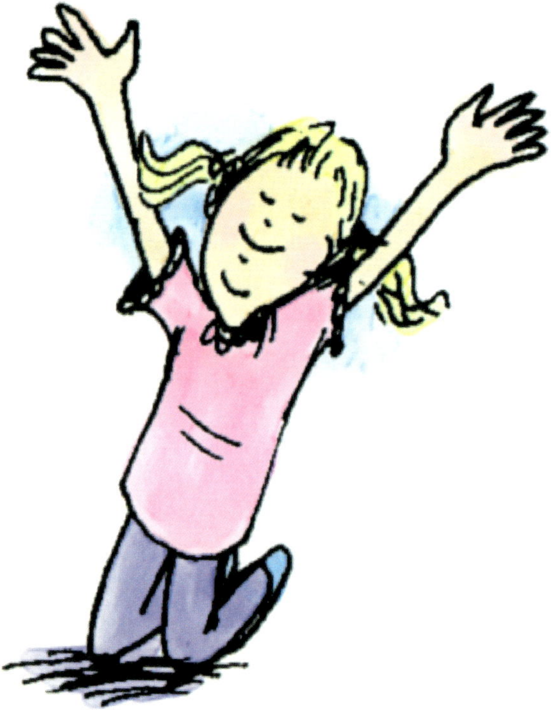

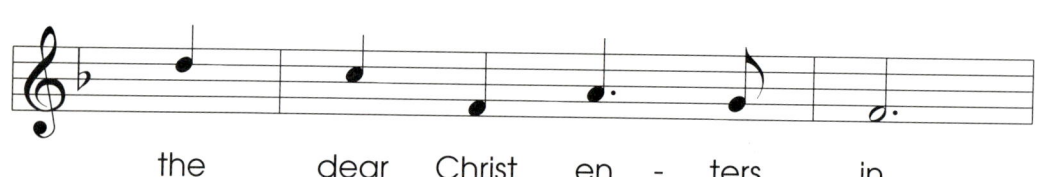

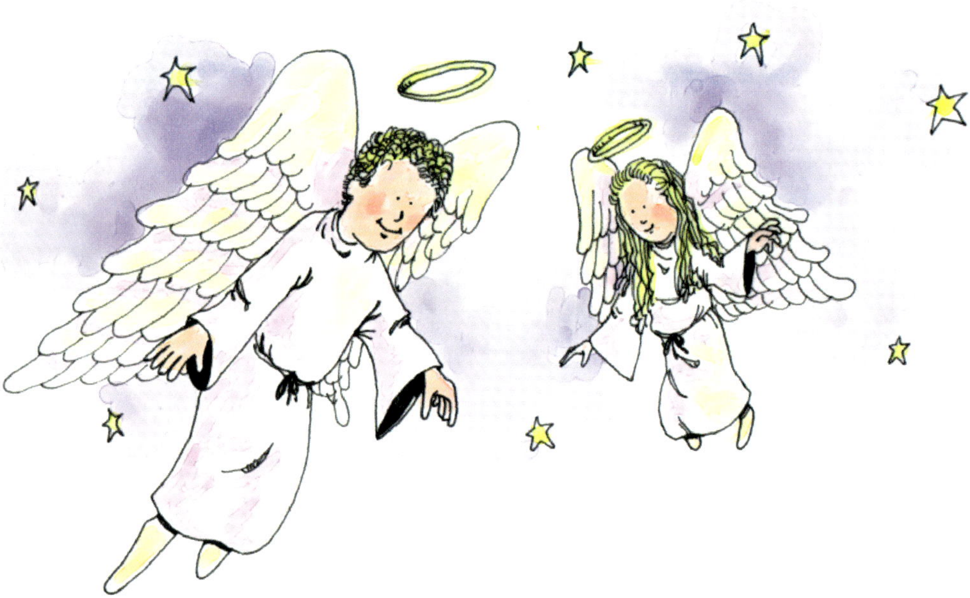

We hear the Christ-mas an- gels the great, glad tid- ings tell.

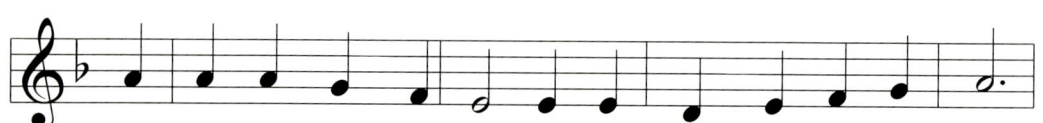

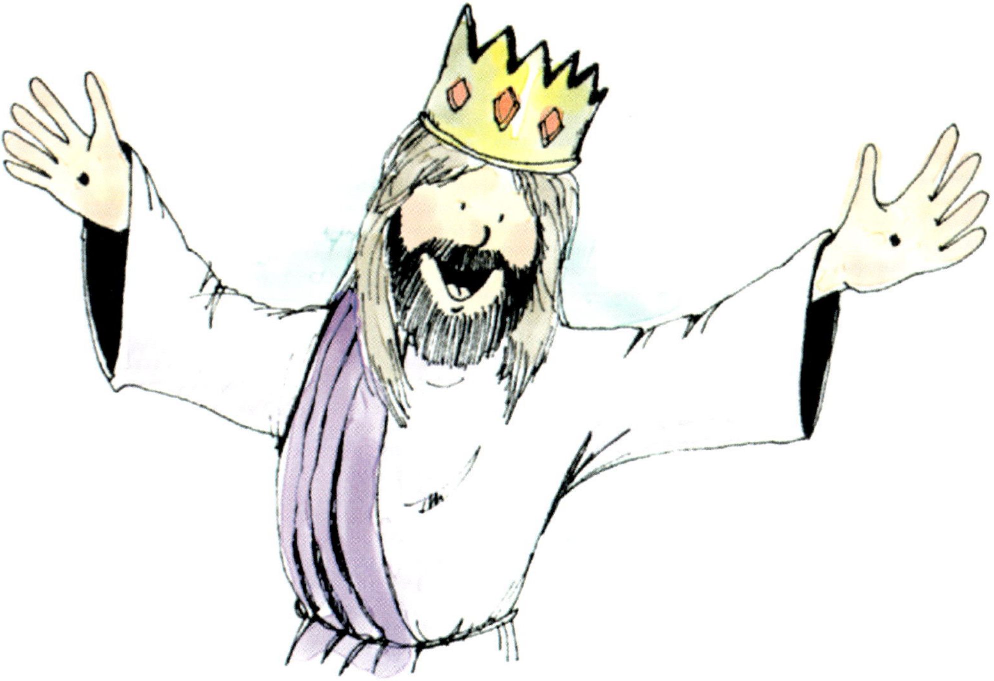

O come to us, a - bide with us, our Lord Em-man- u - el!

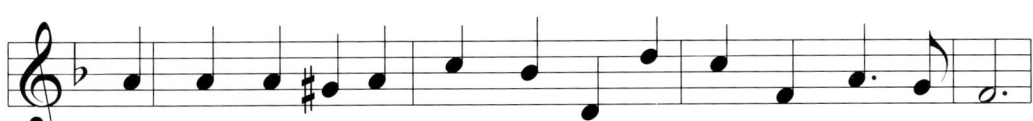